A Perfect Place to Be

Story and Pictures by Bijou Le Tord

Parents' Magazine Press

New York

LIBRARY OF CONGRESS CATALOGING IN PUBLICATION DATA
Le Tord, Bijou.
    A perfect place to be.

    SUMMARY: A hundred or more years ago, Jeremiah M.
Coolin's home atop a hill overlooking the small
village of Hillsley seems the perfect place to be.
    [1. United States—Social life and customs—
19th century—Fiction] I. Title.
PZ7.L568Pe   [E]   75-33098
ISBN 0-8193-0842-0   ISBN 0-8193-0843-9 lib. bdg.

A PERFECT PLACE TO BE

When Jeremiah M. Coolin sits on top of the big hill where he lives, he can see, down below, the village of Hillsley.

It is a perfect place to be.

His house on the hill is sheltered among big old trees
that smell of good wood and thick leaves.

Every Saturday morning Jeremiah M. Coolin takes out the horse
and buggy that his father and he ride together to the
General Store. There they buy all the necessary provisions
for the farm.

Jeremiah M. Coolin has lots of friends down in Hillsley. But this is a special day, for Jeremiah M. Coolin gets to see his favorite friend, Elisha B. Porter, the daughter of Mrs. Porter who owns the General Store.

He likes Elisha B. Porter, not only because she wears a blue-flowered dress, but because she always exchanges candies and apples for some freshly-churned butter that Jeremiah M. Coolin and his father bring.

Something new happens almost every day down in Hillsley.
Sometimes a traveling painter comes from a nearby county
and asks people to pose for him while he paints
their portraits. This particular Saturday, the painter
was drawing a picture of Elisha B. Porter in her back garden
by the raspberry bushes. Jeremiah M. Coolin peeked
through the door. Elisha B. Porter was sitting with her
cat beside her.

Jeremiah M. Coolin decided that he, too, should be part of the painting. They were both excited to see their faces, eyes, noses, hands, painted on a well-smoothed piece of sugar pinewood. It made them look happier and more beautiful than they thought they were.

Mrs. Porter and Mr. Coolin were waiting in the dining room where the artist
had just finished, the day before, two large stencilled walls. Jeremiah M. Coolin
could hardly believe it. Two whole walls of well-shaped painted patterns.
He would ask his mother to hire the painter for their house on the hill.

Main Street has many things to see.

Jeremiah M. Coolin feels so good walking with his father
to Mr. Hartwell's shop. Mr. Hartwell is the father of
Charlotte V. Hartwell, and the wood-carver of Hillsley.

Mr. Hartwell is very skillful at making small wagons and carts out of wood,
as well as brown-and-beige spotted cows, black and white goats, long-necked
geese, and the most handsome cats and horses. Charlotte V. Hartwell
is lucky to have a father who can make her all the toys she wants.

Jeremiah M. Coolin had always wanted a small wooden cart,
especially the red one that had two horses attached to it.
Charlotte V. Hartwell asked if Jeremiah M. Coolin could have it.
Indeed Jeremiah M. Coolin *could* have it, provided he would help
with the making of a quilt next Saturday.

How nice it is, sitting at the Quilting-Bee Party,
cutting, sewing, and putting all the brightly-colored
little pieces of fabric together...

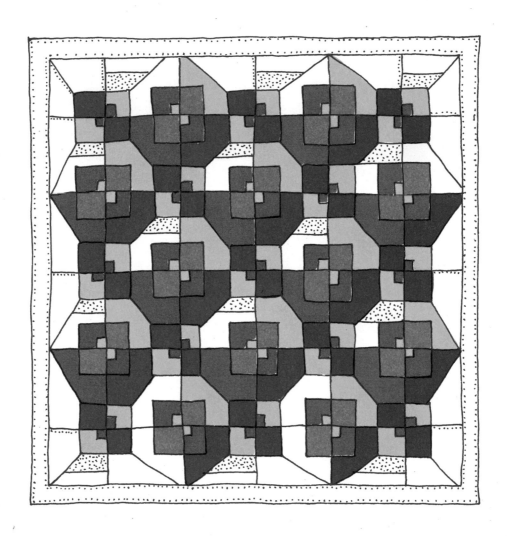

which, in the end, will make a cozy warm cover.

The raspberry pies, oatmeal cookies, hot chocolate and milk,
the cupcakes with raisins, all cover the long oak table that
Mr. Hartwell made for his family when he was not busy
carving toys and weathervanes for the rest of the villagers.

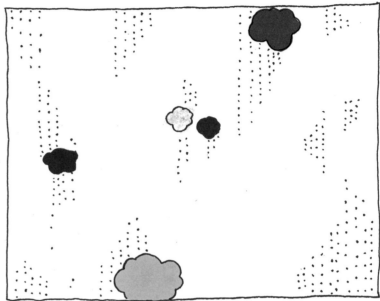

On Jeremiah M. Coolin's birthday, Charlotte V. Hartwell gave him
a horse weathervane, which his father carefully set up on the
roof of the barn.

Each morning Jeremiah M. Coolin runs to the hill and sits and watches
the horse that will tell him all the different winds and rains.

From far away Jeremiah M. Coolin can see heavy gray skies, thick
blue rain, or clouds opening up to a round yellow sun.
Sitting on top of the big hill has taught him a lot. Jeremiah M. Coolin
looks down below. There is the village of Hillsley.

It is a perfect place to be.

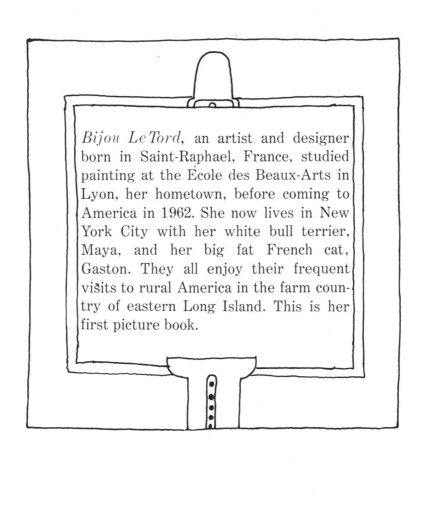

Bijou LeTord, an artist and designer born in Saint-Raphael, France, studied painting at the École des Beaux-Arts in Lyon, her hometown, before coming to America in 1962. She now lives in New York City with her white bull terrier, Maya, and her big fat French cat, Gaston. They all enjoy their frequent visits to rural America in the farm country of eastern Long Island. This is her first picture book.